First published 1992 by Walker Books Ltd
87 Vauxhall Walk, London SE11 5HJ

This edition published 2009

2 4 6 8 10 9 7 5 3 1

© 1992 Nick Sharratt

The right of Nick Sharratt to be identified as author/illustrator of this work has been
asserted by him in accordance with the Copyright, Designs and Patents Act 1988

This book has been typeset in AT Arta

Printed in China

British Library Cataloguing in Publication Data:
a catalogue record for this book is available from the British Library.

ISBN 978-0-7445-2229-7

www.walker.co.uk

The Green Queen

Nick Sharratt

WALKER BOOKS

AND SUBSIDIARIES

LONDON · BOSTON · SYDNEY · AUCKLAND

The
green queen

lay in her
red bed

and looked
at the grey day.

But she had
to go out,
so she got up.

She put
on her blue
shoes,

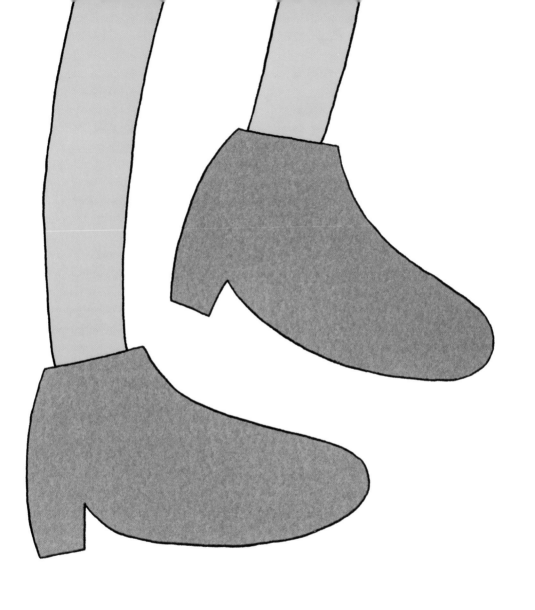

her
black mac,

and her
yellow
and pink
and turquoise
and brown
and orange
and indigo
scarf.
And ...

out she went.